Presented To:

_____

Date:

_____

Grandma's

Memories and Stories

for

Little Girls and Boys

Grandma's Memories and Stories for Little Girls and Boys

New Kids Media™ is published by Baker Book House Company, P.O. Box 6287, Grand Rapids, MI 49516-6287

ISBN 0-8010-4495-2

Scripture is taken from the *Holy Bible*, New Living Translation, copyright © 1996. Used by permission of Tyndale House Publishers, Inc., Wheaton, IL 60189. All rights reserved.

Printed in China

1 2 3 4 5 6 7 — 04 03 02 01

Grandma's
Memories and Stories
for
Little Girls and Boys

Carolyn Larsen

Illustrated by Caron Turk

BAKER
A DIVISION OF
Baker Book House Co

Contents

A letter from Carolyn and Caron . . .

Grandmotherhood is a wonderful time in life. It offers the chance to be involved in the lives of precious grandchildren—sharing love and laughter and passing along the wisdom gained from our own life experiences.

Grandparents come in many forms these days. Some are caregivers to their grandchildren. Some live thousands of miles away and stay in touch via telephone, letters, and e-mail. Whatever your grandmothering situation, we hope that you enjoy sharing the stories in this book with your grandchildren. We hope you take advantage of the journal pages to share a little of your history with your grandchildren. Even if they are too young to appreciate those stories now, someday they will love knowing your history.

Make the most of every moment you share with your grandchildren. Enjoy the present—give them hugs and kisses. Share your past—let them know where you came from and how you grew up. Look to the future, building memories today. Share your faith in God and encourage your precious grandchildren to know him and love him with their whole hearts.

Blessings,

Carolyn and Caron

Baseball Disaster

"Grandma, can I see Grandpa's famous baseball?" Sam asked. He sat on the floor looking al-l-l-l-l the way up to the shelf that held the famous baseball, some trophies, and an autographed Mickey Mantle baseball card.

"That's a very special baseball. A lot of famous old baseball players signed it. You can certainly look at it, but wait until I can sit down with you in a few minutes. Be patient," Grandma said as she ruffled Sam's hair.

But Sam couldn't stop thinking about the baseball. He wanted to see it right now. "Maybe if I get a little closer I can see it better," he said to himself. So Sam pulled a chair over and climbed up on it. He stretched and strained, but he still couldn't see the baseball.

He got four big books from Grandma's bookshelf
and stacked them on the chair, then climbed up and
stood on top of the books. They slipped and slid a little
when Sam reached for the baseball. His fingers just
reached the edge of the shelf.

"Sam, are you being patient?" Grandma called from the other room.

"Uh huh," Sam lied while he looked around for something to put on top of the books. He dragged two sofa pillows over and tried to put them on top of the books.

The books were so high that he could only put one
pillow up. He tossed the second one, trying to land it on
top. It took several tries until it finally landed, a little
crooked, on top of the first pillow. Then, with his tongue
sticking out, Sam started climbing.

He climbed onto the chair, the books, the first pillow, and then the second. He reached for the baseball. "Got it," he said, stretching taller. But just as his finger touched the ball, the pillows slid off the books. Sam grabbed for the edge of the shelf.

The baseball, trophies, and autographed Mickey
Mantle baseball card landed on top of Sam. Grandma
came running. "Sorry, Grandma," Sammy whispered.

"I know, Sam, I know," Grandma sighed. "Let's have a
talk about patience."

Things to Do with Grandma

Bucket Toss
Mickey Mantle was a famous baseball player.
Practice your baseball skills by playing Bucket Toss.
Line up four buckets or plastic bowls, each one a
little farther away from you than the previous one.
Try to toss a small ball into each bowl.

Collection Selection
What do you collect? Tell Grandma about your
collection, especially your favorite pieces. If you
don't have a collection, talk about what you might
like to collect.

Remember
Patience makes life more peaceful.

It is better to be patient than powerful; it is better to
have self-control than to conquer a city.
Proverbs 16:32

Grandma Memories

When I was a little girl, I liked to collect

_____

_____

_____

My favorite piece in my collection was

_____

Now I collect

_____

_____

_____

My favorite childhood hero (for example: athlete, author, musician) was

_____

Super Special Grandma Time

"It's Grandma Day! It's Grandma Day! My super-special Grandma Day!" Hannah sang. Momma brushed her hair into a ponytail and tied a pink ribbon around it. Hannah got dressed and sat in the chair by the living room window watching for Grandma's car.

Hannah's brother and sister were not coming along on her visit with Grandma today. None of her cousins would be there. It was special Grandma time just for Hannah.

Hannah hugged Momma good-bye and waved to her brother and sister. They didn't look very happy. They wanted to come with Grandma, too. But they would have their own special Grandma time on another day.

"What would you like to do today?" Grandma asked.

A million ideas tumbled from Hannah. Grandma said, "Same ideas I had." So Hannah and Grandma set off on their special day. They went to the children's museum and played in the water exhibit all morning. That was Hannah's favorite.

They had lunch in a tearoom with fancy tables and pretty curtains on the windows. Hannah and Grandma both dressed up in old-time clothes and pretended they were princesses.

After lunch they stopped at a park where ducks were swimming in a pond. Hannah tossed bread crusts to them. She giggled and giggled when they came running for more. Grandma took her picture.

Later Hannah asked, "Grandma, what did you want to be when you grew up?"

"When I was your age I wanted to be a nurse. But later I decided that I wanted to help children learn. So I became a teacher. What would you like to be?"

"I want to be an astronaut 'cause it would be fun to float in the air; or a veterinarian so I can play with puppies. Or maybe I'll drive a school bus and be really nice to all the kids," Hannah said.

"Sounds good, but you know what the best thing is, Hannah? You can be anything you want to be!"

Things to Do with Grandma

Bird Lunch
Make a bird feeder by rolling a pine cone in peanut butter, then in bird seed. Hang it from a tree branch and watch the birds (and squirrels) have lunch.

Hide 'N Seek
Play hide 'n seek inside the house or in the backyard.

Remember
Tell someone special how much you care about him or her.

Love each other with genuine affection, and take delight in honoring each other.
Romans 12:10

Grandma Memories

When I was a little girl, these were some of
my favorite things to do

_____

_____

_____

My favorite games to play were

_____

_____

_____

My favorite friends were

_____

_____

_____

My special pet was

_____

_____

_____

Gram's Attic

"Wake up, sleepyhead." Momma shook Natalie's shoulder until she yawned and stretched. "Come on, Sweetheart, time to go to Gram's house." That was all Natalie needed to hear. Tossing back the covers, she slid out of bed.

Sometimes Natalie complained about getting up to go to Gram's house while Momma went to work. But not today! In fact, she dressed by herself and Momma didn't say a word about how her clothes didn't match or that her shoes were on the wrong feet.

"Gram said we're going to do something special today," Natalie told Momma. She was so excited that she could hardly sit still. "We're going up in her attic to look at treasures."

An hour later Natalie helped Gram water her flowers and finish her other morning chores. She was trying her best to be patient. Finally, Gram said, "Well, shall we go up to the attic and see what treasures we can find?"

Gram went right to a big cedar chest and pulled out a worn pink blanket. "This belonged to your mom when she was little. She never let it out of her sight." Gram sounded sad.

"Momma had a blankie?" Natalie had never thought about her mom as a little girl.

"Where did you get this train set?" Natalie asked, lifting an engine out of a box.

"That was Uncle Phil's," Gram answered. "He and your grandpa spent hours playing with it, setting up little towns and making up stories about them." Natalie thought she saw tears in Gram's eyes.

Then Natalie found some pictures of her mom, Gram, Grandpa, and Uncle Phil playing in the snow. Gram found Momma's high school cheerleading uniform and Natalie tried it on.

"What's in that big white box on the shelf?" Natalie asked. Gram pulled it down and lifted out a beautiful dress—Gram's wedding dress.

Now Gram really seemed sad. "Don't be sad," Natalie whispered.

"I'm not, honey, not at all. My wedding dress and all the things from when your mom and Uncle Phil were small make me remember what a wonderful life God has given me. He loves me very much . . . after all, he gave me you!"

Things to Do with Grandma

Memories

Ask Gram to tell you about when your mom (or dad) was young. What did she like to play? Did she ever get in trouble?

Picture Time

Look at picture albums of Gram's family when she was growing up. Then look at ones of mom or dad when they were growing up. Do you look like your mom or dad did at your age?

Remember

Treasure the past, because you can learn much from it.

Love the Lord your God with all your heart, all your soul, and all your strength.
Deuteronomy 6:5

Grandma's Memories

I grew up in

_____

_____

_____

This is what my house looked like

_____

_____

_____

This is how my bedroom looked

_____

_____

_____

The Grumpiest of the Grumpy

Michael was grumpy! Nothing made him happy. At lunchtime Nana made a peanut butter and jelly sandwich cut in funny shapes . . . usually his favorite . . . but not today! "Icky! Yucky! I don't want it!" he shouted. Nana suggested that he go rest in his room.

Michael sat down and grabbed his backpack. It had scissors, tape, markers, and other craft things in it. Michael drew a picture of a thunderstorm with big black clouds and lightning bolts and rain pelting down on a little house.

"This stinks!" he growled, wadding up the paper and throwing it across the room. The black marker fell off his lap and made a mark on the yellow rug. Without even really thinking about it, Michael made another mark . . . then another.

He scooted over to the wall and drew a house and a truck and a tree with the black marker. He was drawing away when Nana came to see if he was feeling any better. "Michael! What are you doing?" Nana couldn't believe her eyes.

Nana knew that something must be wrong, because Michael didn't usually behave like this. "Alright, young man. Sit down and tell me what's going on." Nana used her don't-mess-with-me voice so Michael sat down.

Nana waited, but Michael didn't say anything. "One time my best friend decided she wanted a new best friend," Nana said softly. "Instead of yelling at her, I threw my brother's truck against a tree. He hadn't done anything to me, but I was so angry that I couldn't help myself. Is that kind of what you're feeling today?" she asked.

"Kind of," Michael whispered. "My class is having a party at the park with a picnic and swimming and playground stuff and all the moms and dads are coming," Michael whispered. "I want Mom and Dad to go with me." Tears rolled down his face.

I·LOVE GrANDMA

"I know it's been hard since your mom and dad divorced. But they both love you very much. I love you, too, and I love having you live with me. My goodness, I would be so lonely if you weren't here. If your dad is home from his business trip, I know he will want to come to the party. . . and, if you want, I'd love to come, too."

Things to Do with Grandma

History Walk

Visit a local museum. What can you
learn about the history of the area
where you live?

Snack Time

Make ice cream sundaes with all kinds of
your favorite toppings.

Remember

Thank God for all the people
who love you.

Love one another.
1 John 3:23

Grandma Memories

These were some of my favorites
(song, book, color, flower)

_____

_____

_____

_____

_____

_____

I spent time with these relatives
as a child: aunts, uncles, cousins

_____

_____

_____

_____

_____

_____

_____

One Sticky Grandma

"My head hurts," Noah moaned.

Momma touched her cheek to his forehead. "Hmm, you do feel a little warm," she said. "Why don't you snuggle up here on the couch with Dexter? I'll get some cool water for you." Noah hugged his stuffed dolphin and rested on the couch.

The next morning Noah felt even worse and his temperature was 103. "We're going to see Dr. Smiley this morning," Momma said. Noah felt so bad that he didn't even argue. The doctor checked him over and decided that Noah needed to go to the hospital.

The nurse helped Noah get settled. She even brought a soft, yellow blanket and made a little pillow for Dexter. Noah was glad to have his special friend there with him because the big hospital had different noises and people hurrying around. It was scary.

Noah felt a little better when Grandma and Grandpa came. "How's our boy?" Grandma asked. Noah didn't answer, but big tears rolled down his cheeks. Grandma snuggled up close and whispered silly things in his ear, and pretty soon he was trying to smile.

"Only one person can stay with you tonight," Momma said. "Who do you want to stay?"

"Will you stay with me, Grandma?" Noah whispered.

"I'll be right here. If you need anything, you just call SuperGrandma, OK?" Grandma put a towel around her shoulders and pretended to fly around the room.

After everyone left, Grandma pulled out a bag of stickers. There were stickers of hearts, dogs, stars, flowers, rocket ships, and lots of other things. Grandma put stickers on Noah's cheeks and on Dexter's head. Then she told stories until Noah drifted off to sleep.

The next day Noah gave a sticker to everyone he saw. When it was time to go for an Xray, Grandma sat in the wheelchair and held Noah on her lap. He gave the Xray lady a sticker, too.

"I'll be so happy when you get home that I'll come to your house with stickers all over me!" Grandma told him. Noah giggled. He didn't think she would really do that.

A couple of days later Noah and Dexter came home.
He was glad to be back in his own bedroom. That night
Grandma and Grandpa came to visit. Grandma came in
with stickers on her face, in her hair, on her arms and
legs! "You did it!" Noah cried. "I didn't think you would
do it, but you did it!"

Things to Do with Grandma

Cheer Up Pictures

Use stickers, markers, and crayons to make pretty pictures. Send the pictures to someone who is sick.

Snuggle Time

Watch each of your favorite videos. Snuggle together while you watch. Eat popcorn and drink hot chocolate.

Remember

Laughter makes you feel better . . . no matter what!

A cheerful heart is good medicine.
Proverbs 17:22

HA HA HEE HAA SILLY TALK

Grandma Memories

When I was sick, my mom made me
feel better by

_____

_____

_____

My friends and I used to do
this for fun

_____

_____

_____

_____

_____

_____

HA HA HEE HAA SILLY TALK

Hair Today

Haley has hair just like Grandma's. They have pretty red hair that falls in gentle curls. Haley's hair is long— past her shoulders. Sometimes Grandma brushes Haley's hair into a ponytail. She ties a pretty ribbon around it. Sometimes she puts in colorful barrettes.

Grandma lets Haley brush her short hair sometimes, too. Haley brushes it and puts in barrettes and ribbons and tries to make it look pretty. But for some reason it never seems to look as good as Haley thinks it will.

One morning, Haley got dressed all by herself. She pulled on her favorite purple shirt and the matching shorts with pink flowers. Then she brushed her hair, but some pieces right in the middle on the top of her head were sticking up. As hard as Haley brushed, they wouldn't stay down.

Haley could think of only one way to make it look better. She got the scissors from Momma's bathroom and cut the sticky-out hairs off. She meant to cut just a little bit. But when she was finished, one side was longer than the other. So she cut a little bit off this side, then a little from the other side, trying to make it look better. It didn't.

When Momma came in, she cried, "What are you doing?" She looked down at the soft, red hair on the bathroom floor.

Haley started crying. "I was trying to make it look better, but now my pretty hair is ugly!" The angry look left Momma's face and she hugged her sad girl.

They hurried to Julie's house because she did all of their family's haircuts. Haley climbed up on the big chair and watched in the mirror as Julie trimmed and cut to make her hair even. Big tears rolled down Haley's cheeks as chunks of hair fell to the floor.

When they got home the phone was ringing. It was Grandma. While Momma told her the whole story, Haley hid her head under a pillow and cried. "No one will know this is me. My long hair is gone. I look ugly!"

A while later Grandma came to visit. "Look what I've got!" she said, coming straight to Haley. Opening a bag, she pulled out brand new hairbands and barrettes and clip-in-ribbons. Things to make Haley's short hair look pretty. But Haley's very favorite was a pink barrette with pink and yellow ribbons streaming from it. In fancy yellow paint it said "Haley" right on it!

Things to Do with Grandma

Water Play
Fill the sink with water and play with buckets,
bowls, strainers, and spoons.

Snack Time
Make gelatin squares in your favorite flavors.
Cut them out with cookie cutters.

Remember
When you can cheer someone, you have done
a very good thing.

Loving God means keeping
his commandments.
1 John 5:3

Grandma Memories

When I was young, the most popular
hairstyles were

_____

_____

_____

In my favorite picture of my mom,
she's wearing

_____

_____

_____

One time I really got in trouble for

_____

_____

_____

_____

_____

_____

Things to Do at Grandma's House

Grandma and I make chocolate chip cookies. She shows me how to cream the margarine with the sugar and then mix in all the other things. We each get six chocolate chips to snack on while we're mixing!

Grandma says I am the best singer she has ever heard. So she plays the piano while I sing. Sometimes she sings with me, and we have so much fun that we do a singing parade around the house. Grandpa says we're silly.

When the weather gets warm, Grandma plants a garden. I help her smooth out the ground and dig little holes to drop the seeds in. Later in the summer we'll eat carrots, lettuce, and corn from Grandma's garden.

When a button pops off my jacket, Grandma shows me how to sew it on. I am pretty good at getting the thread in the tiny hole in the needle. Then Grandma helps me put the button back on my coat. It's hard and I have to be very careful with the sharp needle.

On rainy days, we use all the books from my bookshelf and make a book sidewalk around the house. Grandma thinks of the funniest places for the path to go. Then we pretend that the floor is water and we have to stay on the book path.

I like to stand on a chair and watch Grandma cut the
tomatoes and onions to make spaghetti sauce. She shows
me how to toss the spaghetti against the wall. If it sticks
then it's done and ready to eat. If it falls, she has to cook
it some more!

Grandma and I draw funny faces on big brown bags. Grandma's face has big freckles and a silly nose and great big glasses. We cut holes for our eyes and mouths and wear our bag faces all afternoon. It's fun!

When it's time for my nap, Grandma and I snuggle
on the bed and she reads a story. I like the ones about
Jesus and how he helped people. Then Grandma prays
that I'll have a good nap. I'm sure that's why I usually do.

Things to Do with Grandma

Sing Along
Sing silly songs that you both know. Then make up more silly songs.

Puppet Show
Make puppets from brown bags. Draw silly faces on them. Have the puppets sing your silly songs.

Remember
Life is too short to always be serious.

Don't worry about anything; instead, pray about everything. Tell God what you need, and thank him for all he has done.
Philippians 4:6

Grandma Memories

When I was young, I wanted to be a

_____

when I grew up.

Jobs I have had

_____

_____

_____

_____

After graduating from high school, I

_____

_____

_____

Grandma, May I?

Tiffany is used to getting her own way. She thinks that if she pouts or throws a temper tantrum her Momma and Daddy will do whatever she wants. Usually that's exactly what happens.

"I want ice cream!" Tiffany shouts. Momma doesn't go to the freezer right away, so Tiffany falls down on the ground, kicks her feet, and screams, "Ice cream! Ice cream!"

Momma tries sitting Tiffany on the time-out chair. She tries taking away privileges, such as playing with friends or watching videos. Nothing works. Tiffany still gets angry and behaves very badly.

Tiffany spends every Thursday afternoon at Grandma's house while Momma works at her part-time job. This particular Thursday, Tiffany is behaving even more selfishly than usual. "Take me to the park!" she orders.

"You know what, my dear? I think we need to play a game," Grandma says. "I remember a fun game that I played with your mother when she was a little girl. It helped her remember a nice way to ask for things."

"It's called Mother, May I? But since you're playing it with me we'll call it, Grandma, May I? This is how you play. You stand on this line. I'll tell you to take a certain number of steps. Before you do, you must say, 'Grandma, may I?' If you forget, you must go all the way back to the start."

Tiffany and Grandma played all afternoon. Sometimes Tiffany got all the way to the finish line. Then she and Grandma switched places and Grandma had to ask, "Tiffany, may I?" Sometimes Tiffany forgot to ask and she had to go back to the starting line—even if she was nearly finished.

When Grandma had to stop to make dinner, Tiffany said, "I want to watch a video!" Grandma slowly turned around and looked at her. "Oops, I mean, Grandma, may I watch a video?" Tiffany said.

"That's my girl!" Grandma said, giving Tiffany a great big hug.

Things to Do with Grandma

Outdoor Enjoyments

Stretch out on the ground and look up at the sky. Find cloud shapes that make pictures.

Sit outside in the dark and watch the stars. Maybe you'll see a shooting star.

Remember

Treat other people the same way you would like to be treated.

Be kind to each other, tenderhearted, forgiving one another, just as God through Christ has forgiven you.
Ephesians 4:32

Grandma Memories

My best birthday party was
when I was

_____

We had the party at

_____

_____

This is what we did

_____

_____

_____

The best present I ever
received was

_____

_____

_____

A Silly Nilly Grandma

Madeline never knew what to expect when she visited Grandma's house. That's why it was fun to go there. Grandma lived in a yellow house that had blue shutters with cut-out hearts on them. Hearts were perfect for Grandma's house because Grandma was full of love.

90

Madeline and Momma walked up the steps and the door swung open. There was Grandma! She wore a bright blue plastic bowl on her head and big pink sunglasses. "Hello, Princess Madeline! Come in, come in. Your crown and robe are waiting for you."

Madeline giggled and followed Grandma to the kitchen. Her crown was a bright orange strainer and her robe was a red-and-white checked dish towel. "Flowers for you, Princess," Grandma said, placing a bouquet of broccoli in Madeline's arms. Momma put Madeline's overnight bag down, curtsied, and waved good-bye to the princess.

"Tea will be served in the garden," Grandma said in her best British accent. Madeline adjusted her crown and looked around. There wasn't a garden at Grandma's house. What was she talking about? "Follow me, Your Highness," Grandma said, leading the way to the family room.

"Please be seated on your throne and I will serve tea and crumpets." Grandma pointed to an upside-down red plastic bucket. Pots and pots of flowers surrounded it. Madeline sat down. Grandma carried in an upside-down garbage can lid that had juice boxes and fish crackers on it.

Every time Madeline took a drink, her slightly-too-big crown slipped down over her nose. "For dessert, Your Highness, we have your favorite, peanut butter and chocolate syrup." Grandma scooped a little dab of peanut butter and poured chocolate syrup over it before handing it to Madeline.

"Momma doesn't let me have this," Madeline said.

"Well, princesses get to have treats that regular little girls don't," Grandma whispered. "Besides, special things happen at Grandma's house, right?"

"Right!" Madeline giggled.

princesses get special treats...

Grandma made a royal bowling alley with empty soda bottles and Madeline rolled an orange to knock them all down. Then they went into the royal theatre and watched a movie. The whole evening was one royal surprise after another in the palace of a very special, kind of silly grandma.

Things to Do with Grandma

Windows of Love

Cut various sizes of hearts from many different colors of paper. Decorate the windows with them.

Have a Tea Party

Make a crown and robe for each of you to wear. Serve your favorite kind of tea and crackers or cookies.

Remember

The things you do today make the memories of tomorrow.

For God so loved the world that he gave his only Son, so that everyone who believes in him will not perish but have eternal life.

John 3:16

Grandma Memories

Believe it or not, I remember
a time before

_____

was invented.

This is what we used instead

_____

_____

_____

The first car I remember my
parents driving was a

_____

Secret Gifts

Momma sat down on Kelsey's bed and said, "Kels, we have to talk. I know Grandma is very special to you so I think you should know that she's going to the hospital in a couple of days. She is going to have an operation on her heart. The doctors will take very good care of her."

Kelsey softly asked, "Could I go see Grandma tomorrow?"

"I think that would be a good idea," Momma said. "How about if we say a little prayer for Grandma right now?"

Momma knelt down beside her and Kelsey prayed, "Dear God, please take care of Grandma. I love her lots. Amen."

Kelsey was up bright and early the next morning. Momma could hear her scurrying around in her room. When she came down for breakfast Kelsey was carrying her favorite bright pink backpack. It had a picture of a little kitten on it.

"What have you got there?" Momma asked.

"Just some stuff for Grandma," Kelsey answered. After breakfast Momma drove Kelsey to Grandma's house. She ran some errands while Kelsey and Grandma visited.

Grandma could tell Kelsey was worried. "Don't worry, we'll soon be drinking lemonade on the patio, just like last summer," Grandma assured her.

"I'll come and water your flowers every day and take care of Butter (that was Grandma's cat). I'll do all the stuff that you don't feel like doing, okay?" Kelsey said.

"I appreciate your help," Grandma said. "What's in your backpack?"

Kelsey suddenly got a little bit shy. "Well, umm, just some things to help you get well. Don't open it until you get to the hospital, okay?" Kelsey made Grandma promise.

When Grandma checked into the hospital, she opened the pink backpack. What she found inside made her cry: a hand-drawn heart with a bright red, "I love you" in the middle; Kelsey's favorite stuffed teddy bear, worn and stained from being loved so much; and Grandma's favorite kind of red lollipop.

Grandma's best cookies...

Grandma's kitty ♥ Butter

Grandma's favorite Sucker

I Love Grandma

Most special of all, there was a picture of Kelsey. Grandma looked at Kelsey's smiling face and knew how special these things were. They were some of Kelsey's favorite things and some of Grandma's favorite things. Grandma smiled because she knew how much Kelsey loved her.

Things to Do with Grandma

Looking at Memories

Look around Grandma's attic or in boxes of things she kept from her youth or your mom or dad's youth. What special things do you find?

Cooling Off

On a hot day, paint with water on the driveway. Pour a bucket of water on the driveway and brush the water around with a broom.

Remember

Keep busy, but don't forget to take a rest once in a while.

Draw close to God, and God will draw close to you.
James 4:8

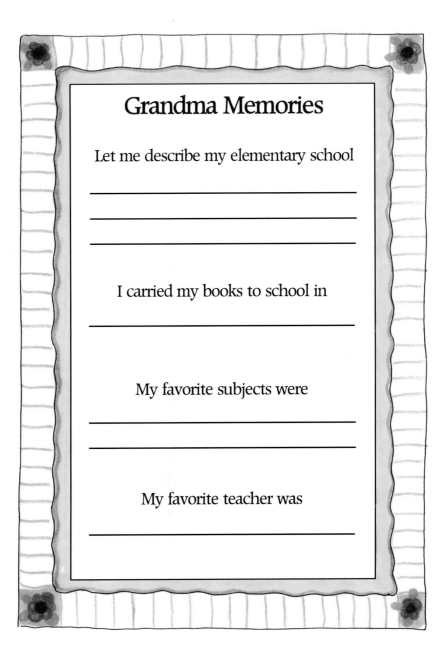

Grandma Memories

Let me describe my elementary school

_____

_____

_____

I carried my books to school in

_____

My favorite subjects were

_____

_____

My favorite teacher was

_____

On the Road

Grandma had a good tradition. When all of her grandchildren reached the ripe old age of eight years, she took them on a private vacation with her. Andrew thought this was a pretty good tradition because he would be eight years old next week. He couldn't wait to hear what she had planned for him.

Andrew's older brother, Travis, went to a dude ranch in Colorado with Grandma. His cousin Catherine went to Disney World. Grandma seemed to know exactly what each of her grandchildren would enjoy.

Mom made Andrew's favorite dinner for his birthday. Grandma came and they all ate spaghetti, garlic bread, and fruit salad. Then Mom brought out the chocolate birthday cake with eight candles on it. After Andrew opened his other presents, Grandma handed him a card.

It read, "I love how kind and helpful you are. For your trip I would like you to join me on a missions trip to Mexico. We'll help the missionaries build a new orphanage. You can also play with the children who will live in the new house. Next, we will go to a resort near the ocean and play in the sand and enjoy the sunshine. Love, Grandma."

"Cool," Andrew said. A few short weeks later Andrew and Grandma and thirty other people were working away on the house for the orphans. Sometimes Andrew carried buckets of nails or planks of wood. Sometimes he got to hammer the nails.

When he got tired of working, Andrew went to the house where the orphans were staying and played soccer with them. Even though they didn't speak the same language, they had lots of fun. He became friends with Julio, a boy about his own age.

When it was time for the workers to go home, Andrew was sad to leave. It was fun to be part of the missionaries' work and to get to know the children. One of the missionaries said that she would translate his letters into Spanish if he wanted to write Julio.

The beach days were lots of fun, too. Andrew saw dolphins and a jellyfish. He and Grandma built sand castles. But the part of the trip he would always remember was working on the orphanage in Mexico . . . and playing with Julio.

Things to Do with Grandma

Making Good Use of Time
Volunteer together at a local food pantry or homeless shelter

Just for Fun
Make paper airplanes and have contests to see whose flies the farthest.

On Parade
Use pots/pans and wooden spoons for instruments. Do a musical parade through the house.

Remember
No matter where you go, it's always good to come home.

We love each other as a result of his loving us first.
1 John 4:19

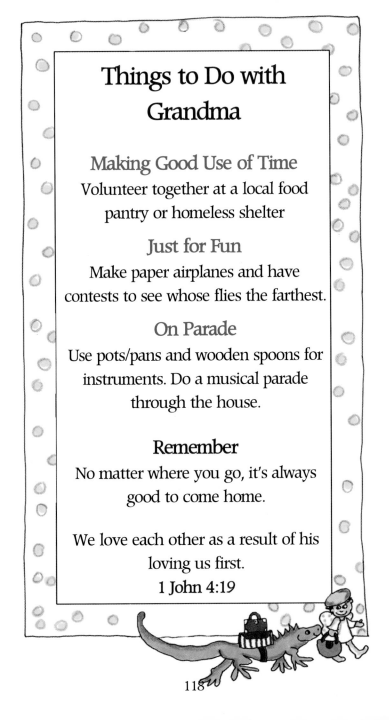

118

Grandma Memories

My mom and dad were from

_____

_____

_____

My best memories of them are

_____

_____

_____

_____

_____

Our family went to church at

_____

_____

_____

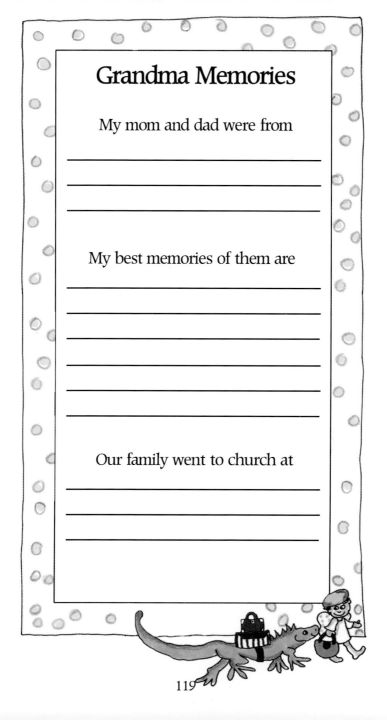

Grandparents' Day

"Next Thursday is Grandparents' Day at school. Can Grandma come?" asked Heather.

Mom put down her book and pulled Heather onto her lap. "I know she would love to come. But she lives very far away. It would be a long plane ride and cost lots of money for Grandma to come next week. I'm sorry, but I don't think Grandma can come."

"But we're learning special songs and we're doing a play. Then the grandparents are going to eat lunch with us. All the other kids will have a grandma there. Some will even have a grandpa, too," Heather said.

"I have an idea," Mom said. "You know Mrs. Barker across the street? Well, her grandchildren all live far away. That means she can't go to Grandparents' Day at their schools. What would you think of inviting her to be your adopted grandma for next week?"

At first Heather didn't like Mom's idea. But then she thought about Mrs. Barker missing Grandparents' Day with her own grandkids. She thought about how nice Mrs. Barker was and how she gave Heather presents on her birthday and lemonade on hot days.

So with Mom's permission, Heather crossed the street to invite Mrs. Barker. She explained about Grandparents' Day and asked Mrs. Barker to be her adopted grandma. "Heather, I would love to be your adopted grandma," Mrs. Barker said. She really seemed happy.

All Thursday morning Heather had a hard time
paying attention to the teacher. She couldn't wait for the
program. At eleven o'clock the grandparents began
coming. Mrs. Barker was right on time. The grandparents
sat down and the students sang their songs and
performed their play.

When the program was over the students and their grandparents enjoyed a lunch served by some of the moms. Heather sat beside Mrs. Barker. "Thanks for coming, Mrs. Barker. I like having an adopted grandma," Heather said.

Dear Mrs. Barker,
Thank you for
being my adopted
grandma.
Love,
Heather xoxo

"Well, thank you for inviting me, Heather. I miss my grandchildren, so it's nice to get to share this day with you." Mrs. Barker said. "I would like it if you call me anytime you need a grandma. When I want to spend some time with my adopted granddaughter, can I call you?" Heather thought that was a very good idea.

Things to Do with Grandma

Sharing the Joy

Think of an older woman who doesn't have grandchildren around. How can you be friends with her?

A Cool Treat

Make juice popsicles by pouring your favorite juice into small paper cups. Freeze them. Then tear the paper down a little at a time and enjoy.

Remember

It's better to show love with actions than with words.

Think of ways to encourage one another to outbursts of love and good deeds.
Hebrews 10:24

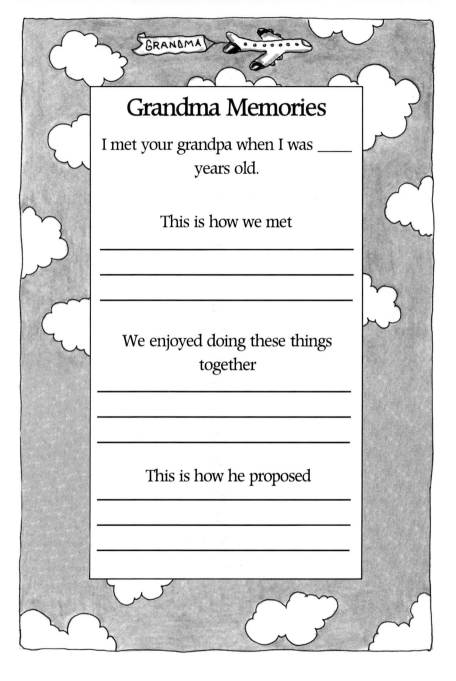

Grandma Memories

I met your grandpa when I was ____ years old.

This is how we met

_____

_____

_____

We enjoyed doing these things together

_____

_____

_____

This is how he proposed

_____

_____

_____

What a God We Have!

Matthew spent the summer at Grandma's farm. He was a big help to Grandma. He fed the chickens and gathered the eggs. Every time he brought them inside Grandma said, "Aren't eggs a miracle, Matthew? What a God we have!"

Grandma always planted a big garden. Matthew helped her by dropping seeds into the ground. Then he turned the hose on every morning to water the seeds. When the little plants started growing, Grandma said, "Look at them pushing that dirt out of the way, Matthew. What a God we have!"

There was a little cabin in the woods near Grandma's house. She and Matthew slept there sometimes. Before they went to bed, they looked at the millions of stars in the sky. Matthew even saw a shooting star. "Look at that sky, Matthew. What a God we have!" Grandma said.

One evening Matthew and Grandma were walking in the woods when he smelled something yucky. "Over here," Grandma whispered. They climbed up on a big rock and stayed very still while a fat skunk waddled by. "Isn't it amazing that skunks can protect themselves by spraying smelly perfume? What a God we have!" Grandma said.

Grandma hung her laundry out on a clothesline to dry. While she was doing that Matthew laid on the ground and watched some ants running around. "Grandma, come see this ant," Matthew called. It was carrying a cookie crumb that was bigger than it was. "Ants are very strong, aren't they?" Grandma said. "What a God we have!"

134

Crashing thunder woke Matthew in the middle of the night. Lightning zigzagged across the sky. Grandma came in and said, "Let's go sit on the front porch." Each time the lightning flashed, Matthew saw clouds zipping across the sky. "Listen to that thunder and look at the powerful lightning," Grandma said. "What a God we have!"

Late in the summer Grandma's beagle, Nellie, had six puppies. Grandma and Matthew watched the puppies be born. Nellie licked them clean and the puppies snuggled close to her. "Look at those little things. They don't even have their eyes open," Grandma said. "What a God we have."

"God made some powerful things like thunderstorms and some little things like puppies," Matthew said.

"Do you know what my favorite thing is that God made?" Grandma asked.

Matthew didn't know, so Grandma said, "You, Matthew! What a God we have!"

Things to Do with Grandma

Saying Thanks

Make a list of your favorite things that God made.

The Incredible Egg

Boil some eggs until they are cooked.
Decorate them with markers.
Have Grandma show you how to peel off the shell without breaking the egg.

Remember

Be happy with what you have instead of always wanting something else.

O LORD, our Lord, the majesty of your name fills the earth!
Psalm 8:9

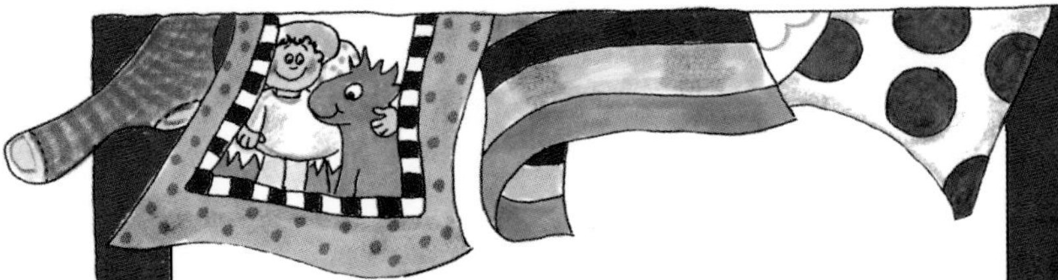

Grandma Memories

Our wedding was

_____

_____

_____

Our honeymoon was to

_____

_____

_____

Our first home was in

_____

_____

_____

You Are Special

Megan crawled under the big mulberry bush in Grandma's backyard. It was her secret hiding place. She could look out through the branches and see what was happening, but no one could see her. This was where she came when something was bothering her.

"Megan. Megan, are you out here?" Grandma knew she was. Grandma even knew where the secret hiding place was. She crawled under the branches and sat down by Megan. "So, what's going on, kiddo? You've been very quiet all day," Grandma said.

"Grandma, am I pretty?" Megan asked. There were tear stains on her cheeks.

"You are the prettiest little girl ever," Grandma said. "Why are you thinking about that?"

Megan didn't answer. She had another question: "Am I dumb?"

"Well, when we played a game last night, you won. Plus, you do math and read books. You get good grades in school. You are certainly not dumb," Grandma said.

"I think I'm boring," Megan said. "I can't do anything like sing or play the piano."

"But you draw pretty pictures. You're good at playing with younger children and you're a good friend," Grandma said.

"Now why don't you tell me what's going on,"
Grandma said. Megan was usually happy and laughing.
What could be making her so unhappy?

"Teacher gave out end-of-the-year awards today. Kallie got one because she plays the piano so good. Tim got one because he's good at sports. Sarah got one because of her good grades," Megan said. "I can't do anything, and I'm not the smartest . . ."

"Remember when you made a get well card for me? It was beautiful," Grandma said. "And how you write notes to encourage your friends? You help me with my garden, and your flowers are always lovely. You're a good cook, too. Don't compare yourself with others, Megan. Be happy with how God made you, because you're special!"

Things to Do with Grandma

Special You

Make an acrostic with your name by using each letter as the first letter of a word that describes you.

C ute
O utgoing
R eally happy
I nspirational

Remember

God made you just the way he wants you to be!

Thank you for making me so wonderfully complex! Your workmanship is marvelous.
Psalm 139:14

Grandma Memories

When I found out I was going to
be a mom, I

_____

_____

We chose the name

_____

for our baby. It means

_____

The baby's room was decorated
with this theme

_____

_____

_____

The Christmas Angel

Christmas meant a trip to Grandma's house. Cori, Mallory, and Ryan looked forward to piling in the van with their dog and riding through the snow to Grandma's house. They sang songs and played games as they traveled. But the trip seemed to take forever.

For weeks before Christmas Grandma baked cookies and made candy. There was candy everywhere! Cori loved the chocolate-covered peanut butter balls. Mallory liked the chow mein noodle candy, and Ryan loved the puppy chow!

Grandma's Christmas tree filled one whole corner of the family room. An electric train circled on the floor underneath it. Presents were piled high all around the train. The kids loved the twinkling lights, and each of them had favorite ornaments on Grandma's tree.

Cori's favorite ornament was the beautiful golden angel that was always on the top of Grandma's Christmas tree. It had a light in it, so it showered a warm light over the whole tree. As their van drove into the driveway, Cori strained to see the angel through the window. It wasn't there!

Grandma told the children that when she got the Christmas things out this year, the angel was broken. "I miss her. That angel topped our family Christmas tree for the last thirty years. After all, the angels played a big part in the first Christmas."

For the next few days everyone was busy with the final preparations for Christmas. There was shopping to finish, cookies to decorate, and snow to play in. But Cori, Mallory, and Ryan were busy planning a secret.

Every afternoon the three of them hid away in a back bedroom. They whispered and giggled and worked on making a new angel for Grandma's tree. They wanted it to look like the angel Grandma used to have. When they were happy with what they had, Dad put a light inside it so it would glow like the old one.

Christmas morning Grandpa read the Christmas
story from the Bible and thanked God for baby Jesus.
Then Cori gave a beautiful package to Grandma. When
she opened it and found the new angel, made with love
just for her . . . well, you know what she did . . . she cried.

Things to Do with Grandma

Christmas Pictures

Cut out pictures from old Christmas cards and use them to make special pictures or cards for someone.

Cookie Time

Even if it isn't Christmastime, bake Christmas shaped cookies and decorate them.

Remember

Thank God every day for the gift of Jesus.

Do for others what you would like them to do for you.
Matthew 7:12

Grandma Memories

My favorite holiday is

_____

I like it because

_____

_____

_____

The way my family celebrated this
holiday was

_____

_____

_____

Describe special ornaments on your
Christmas tree and tell why they are special.

_____

_____

_____

Grandmas, Grandmas, Everywhere

Every grandma is different.

Some grandmas wear business suits and carry briefcases. They ride the commuter train to go to work in the city every day.

Other grandmas live on a farm. They scatter feed for chickens, gather eggs, and drive big tractors in the field.

Some grandmas travel all around the world. They send postcards from England and Switzerland or bring funny presents from Africa.

Other grandmas live in the same house their whole lives. They grow pretty flowers and bake melt-in-your-mouth cookies.

Some grandmas are tall and thin. They do aerobics, ride bikes, and zoom across a lake in a beautiful sailboat.

Other grandmas sit in the backyard swing and look at the night sky. They can point out the Big Dipper and Orion's Belt.

Some grandmas like to be silly and wear a pan on their heads or put their clothes on inside out. Other grandmas are soft and cuddly, and it feels good to curl up next to them and read a book.

There are all kinds of grandmas. But do ypu know who the absolute-very-best-most-special-grandma in the whole world is? MINE!

Thank you, God, for my grandma!

Things to Do with Grandma

Nature Walk

Go for a walk together. Look for different kinds of bugs. Look at different flowers and trees. If it's wintertime, make snowballs and build a snow fort.

Cake Date

Bake a cake together. Decorate it with frosting, sprinkles, and candies.

Remember

Every person is different. That's what makes each of us special!

There is only one Lord, one faith, one baptism, and there is only one God and Father, who is over us all and in us all and living through us all.
Ephesians 4:5-6

Grandma Memories

My grandma lived

_____

_____

_____

My favorite thing about visiting her was

_____

_____

_____

_____

_____

The best thing my grandma cooked was

_____

_____

_____

_____

_____

Long-Distance Grandma

Tears dripped on Ryan's shoes. He took a deep breath and tried to stop crying, but he couldn't. Ryan was even too sad to look at the airplanes parked outside the window. "Grandma, I don't want you to leave. If you'll stay here, you can have my room."

"You're a sweetheart, Ryan. I don't want to go either. I'm going to miss you so much!" Grandma said. She gave him a big hug. "I promise that I will find some way to stay in touch with you. A new way every week, Okay?"

Ryan just had time to nod before Grandma got on the airplane. He pressed his nose against the window and watched until the plane was out of sight. Back at home Ryan thought everything seemed sad now that Grandma's laughter and funny songs were gone.

A few days later a letter came for Ryan. Inside was a half-drawn picture of a clown's face and a note from Grandma. "Dear Ryan, I'm thinking of being a clown at our fall festival. But I can't decide how I want my clown face to look. Could you help me think of one? Love, Grandma."

Ryan got out his markers and had great fun finishing the clown face to look extra happy—just like Grandma! He sent it back to her with a note that said, "I think your clown name should be Giggles, because you always make me laugh!"

A few days later Grandma sent a letter that had the first part of a story in it. She asked Ryan to think of the next thing after, "Tommy and his dog, Boffo, were hiking in the woods. They heard someone crying and when they looked around, they saw . . ."

Ryan had lots of ideas for the story. For the next couple of weeks, he and Grandma sent ideas back and forth. Pretty soon, their story was eight exciting pages long. Ryan drew pictures to go on every page.

Of course, Grandma sent a present for Ryan's birthday. She sent candy for Valentine's Day and a book about Jesus at Easter. Ryan looked forward to the mail coming to see if there was a surprise package from his long-distance grandma. Before he knew it, it was time for Grandma to visit again! "Wow!" he thought. "That went fast thanks to Grandma's great ideas on how to stay in touch!"

Things to Do with Grandma

Staying in Touch
Learn Grandma's phone number
or e-mail address.

Walking on Water
Lay out a magazine sidewalk through the
house. Pretend that every other part of the floor
is water and walk through the house on your
special sidewalk.

Special Plans
Plan and prepare a special dinner for your mom
and dad (with Grandma's help, of course).

Remember
You can be out of a loved one's sight, but
you're never out of their heart.

Nothing in all creation will ever be able to
separate us from the love of God.
Romans 8:39

Grandma Memories

Here are some of my memories of childhood
family vacations

_____

_____

_____

_____

_____

_____

The best trip/vacation I ever went on was to

_____

_____

_____

It was special because

_____

_____

_____

_____

_____

Grandma to the Rescue

Mom didn't feel like playing these days. The baby in her tummy made her tired all the time. So Jacob just played by himself with his toys or looked at pictures in his books. Mom kept saying, "Play quietly," or "Use your inside voice."

"I'm bored!" Jacob shouted one day. "There's nothing to do! There's no one to play with!" He thought that he didn't like the baby in Mom's tummy so much. "Who needs a dumb old baby anyway?" Then, one afternoon, the doorbell rang. It was Grandma!

"Jacob," she said, "I think you need to get out of the house for a while. Let's go for a drive!" Jacob grabbed his coat and ran to Grandma's car. "Now," Grandma said, "I know just what we should do this afternoon." Jacob thought she would suggest a museum or the library.

He could hardly believe it when Grandma said, "Let's go to Jump 'n Go." Three big rooms filled with ball pools and big pipes hanging from the ceiling—big enough for people to crawl through. Jacob climbed up a big net to the pipes and soon he was crawling through them, squeezing past other kids and sliding into the ball pools.

One time Jacob looked down just in time to see Grandma slide into the balls! Grandma was playing in the pipes! At lunchtime Jacob and Grandma shared a cheese pizza and told each other silly stories.

Then Grandma pulled some bubble gum out of her pocket. They had a contest to see who could blow the biggest bubble! Jacob won when Grandma's bubble popped and stuck to her cheeks and glasses. She thought that was funny! What a cool grandma!

They went to Grandma's house to rest, but instead of going inside, Grandma started rolling a snowball. It got bigger and bigger. Jacob made one, too. Soon there was a snowman standing guard in the front yard. Grandma ran in the house and came back with red food coloring to make his cheeks rosy.

On the way home Jacob told Grandma that the day had been fun. "It's kind of hard that Mom can't play with you, isn't it?" Grandma said.

"Yeah," Jacob said. "I miss playing with her."

"I'm sure she misses playing with you, too. But after the baby is born Mom can play again . . . and you'll have the new baby to help with, too." Jacob had forgotten—he was going to have lots of work to do as the brand-new big brother!

Things to Do with Grandma

Playing Inside
Go to an indoor playground and play in the ball pit and climb through the tunnels.

Bubble Catcher
Blow soap bubbles and try to catch them as they float through the air.

Remember
Thinking about other people first makes your own problems seem smaller.

Don't think only of your own good.
1 Corinthians 10:24

Grandma Memories

I had ____ brothers and sisters. Let me
tell you about them.

_____

_____

_____

_____

_____

We used to argue and fight about

_____

_____

_____

_____

We had so much fun when we

_____

_____

_____